I0538327

See You Next Christmas

A Novella

Luisa Cisterna

Copyright © 2025 by Luisa Cisterna

All rights reserved.

No portion of this book may be reproduced in any form without written permission from the publisher or author.

ISBN: 978-1-0698347-1-3

Library and Archives Canada

Cover Design: Benjamim Cesar

Books by the Author

T hank you for purchasing this book! If you enjoy small-town, heartwarming stories of faith and second changes, please see my other books.

God bless you!

Luisa Cisterna

Love Always Protects — A Grace Harbor Series
Love Always Trusts — A Grace Harbor Series

Contents

1. The Stalker

A *ppearances can be deceiving, and rushing into things only wears a person down. This is about my best story.*

Just wait. My best story did not begin with a weirdo. The stalker who haunted my days ended up nudging me straight into the best chapter of my life. I can barely stand to say his name, so let's call him P.F.—short for *Please Forget*.

P.F. was my boyfriend.

Yes. I admit it. Loneliness can throw us into some questionable decisions.

I had just moved to a tiny town of half a thousand people tucked in Western Canada, a place where time seemed to have curled up for a long nap. All seemed silent during the winter months.

And silence can be a torment when you're already feeling hollow.

As a veterinarian, I'd moved there to gain hands-on experience with large animals: horses, cows, alpacas. The clinic I'd worked at in Vancouver was struggling financially, and I figured branching out might open better doors. I was right. Within a year, I was treating livestock for half the ranchers in the region.

And that's when P.F. appeared.

He seemed harmless at first. Nice, even. He owned a handful of equine-supply stores across the foothills, and our shared love for animals pulled us into the same circles. He had that easygoing prairie-cowboy look with scuffed boots, cowboy hat, and a lopsided grin that girls found charming. I did, too.

But beneath all that? A streak of possessiveness I didn't see coming.

Well, bless my poor judgment! I couldn't take a single step without him asking where I was going, who I'd be seeing, when I'd be back. He clung to me like gum stuck to the heel of a boot, the kind you tug and tug, but there's always that stubborn piece that refuses to come off.

We lasted a few weeks before I ended the gum-on-heel relationship. That's when the begging began.

"Baby, don't leave me."

How I hated that *baby*.

"My name isn't Baby. It's Sabrina," I'd remind him.

But he'd just whine, "Sabrina Baby, don't leave me."

Even if every woman in town swooned over him, who could put up with that? I was convinced he had unresolved mother issues, something leaning uncomfortably close to Oedipal. He'd tell me I reminded him of his late mom. It gave me the creeps.

Had he been auditioning for a Hitchcock reboot, playing the Alberta version of Norman Bates?

"Baby, your brown hair falling down your back... your honey eyes... your strong workin' body..."

Strong workin' body? What the...?

Bile shot straight up my throat.

A *strong body for work*? What was I? Livestock? A draft horse? Should I start answering to "Easy, girl"?

I'd study myself in the mirror, relieved to see I looked fit, though yes, my full hips did tend to catch the attention of some cowboys. Still, I was no mare.

The more time passed, the more dread tightened around my ribs. My life started feeling smaller, darker, as if he were drawing the walls in around me. No matter where I went, he turned up, watching me vaccinate horses, leaning on fences while I delivered piglets, showing up at barns with a thermos and two mugs.

"Sabrina Baby, let's have coffee. I'm taking care of you."

Clients noticed my tension long before I realized I wasn't hiding it anymore. A well-connected woman in the equestrian world urged me to call the police.

But what would I tell them?

P.F. never touched me. Never threatened me. Never raised his voice. His sweet words gave me cavities.

The problem? He was just... *there.* All. The. Time.

Always there.

Gum on a cowgirl boot.

It became painfully clear: I needed to leave.

I loved my work, but I needed distance. Miles and moun-tain-ranges of distance from P.F., enough space for three na-tional parks and a few grizzlies in between for extra security.

He followed me on social media too. I had an Instagram ac-count with cute pictures of animals. Mostly cats. To disappear, I'd have to wipe everything. Delete, deactivate, basically ghost the internet so hard even the algorithm would file a missing-per-sons report.

The only safe option. Far.

All the way to my brother Lorenzo's place in Whistler, more than a thousand kilometers of road, mountains, and breathing room between me and P.F. From there, I could finally exhale. Begin again. Search for work with a clear mind and a quieter heart. And until I found my footing, Lorenzo's café would be a safe harbor. Winter would soon settle over the village, bringing its familiar rush of snow, holiday lights, and tourists passing by; life moving at a rhythm I hoped might steady me too.

By the end of November, I called Lorenzo and told him what was going on. Protective as ever, he was horrified. He insist-ed—borderline ordered—that I leave immediately. Change my number. Shut down my social media accounts. Lorenzo had always been that way with me, steady, loyal, the kind of brother who steps in without hesitation when my world starts to wob-ble.

So, I promised him I would leave as soon as I packed and notified my clients.

He also confirmed he needed someone to manage the café. His manager was on maternity leave. I already knew the ropes.

Through college, Lorenzo's café jobs had kept me afloat. Summer work saved for tuition and rent.

After a long talk, I told him I'd need about two weeks to close things out with my clients. I knew they'd understand. None of them approved of how P.F. hovered over me.

Over the next weeks, I shut down everything: social media, phone number, home. I returned my furnished rental, packed my SUV with the pieces of my life, and drove west until the landscape turned white and the air sharp with cold. The Rockies rose ahead of me as I followed the Trans-Canada highway. Somewhere near Revelstoke, the snow thickened into a full curtain, and traffic crawled to a halt for an hour while a plow cleared the pass. I didn't mind. The delay felt almost symbolic, as if life was giving me one last moment to think of what I left behind before I crossed into something new.

I kept going, descending slowly toward the greener stretch of the Lower Mainland, where rain replaced snow and the air softened with the smell of cedar and damp earth. But it wasn't the end of the journey. From there, I climbed north again, following the twisting mountain highway toward Whistler, toward Lorenzo, toward safety, toward the life I hoped was waiting for me on the other side of all that distance.

I didn't know it then, but fleeing that tiny prairie town set me on the road toward my greatest story, toward the place where destiny had quietly been waiting for me all along.

And that was truly the beginning of my best story.

2. The Encounter

What we're not looking for can sometimes end up being the start of a good story.

I arrived at Lorenzo's place yesterday. We were already well into December. He insisted I take a couple of days to rest and unwind before helping at the café, but I told him I needed to stay busy. Truth be told, I woke up tired this morning. My brother and I had stayed up half the night talking. It was worth every yawn today. Finally saying everything out loud, and having Lorenzo respond with the right mix of comfort, common sense, and big-brother encouragement, felt like someone handing me my strength back.

We agreed not to tell our parents I'd quit my job and moved to Whistler for a while. They always worried too much, and deep down I think they still felt guilty for retiring to Florida in true snowbird style and leaving us behind. My mom especially. She could turn a tiny inconvenience into a full-blown family tragedy in under five minutes. My dad was more relaxed, but he called often, asking for "updates," which was just code for "your mother is pacing holes in the carpet." So, the drama could wait.

I'd have to figure out what to tell them about my sudden move. Later. When I changed my phone number, I told them my old one had been cloned. Mom poured out a long list of warnings but didn't question it. She just handed me an hour's worth of warnings, then launched straight into the saga of Aunt Lucy, who "lost all her money to a scammer." I just kept saying "mm-hmm," fully aware this story was Mom's gentle way of avoiding the truth: Aunt Lucy had a shopping problem that could empty any bank account.

After I got dressed, Lorenzo knocked on my door. He said he was heading to the café and would wait for me there. I used the time to unpack and put away my clothes. The apartment had two bedrooms and a cozy living room. The three-story building looked like something out of every cozy mountain village with thick log walls, stone trimming around the base, and balconies dusted with snow. My bedroom window faced the mountains, where the ski lift climbed toward the slopes. It was still dark outside, and the village hadn't quite come alive yet.

Still, I felt excited, although tired. First day. Light snow. Lots of customers.

I finished organizing my things, pulled on my boots and coat, tugged my pink pom-pom toque over my ears, and headed out. Two blocks later, I reached the row of souvenir shops, bistros, and cafés. That would be my world for the next few weeks.

Lorenzo's "Aroma" van sat at the curb with the back doors open. A young guy with pierced ears was loading cardboard boxes into it. I picked up my pace. Mornings were busy. All the corporate holiday events meant extra breakfast deliveries. Lots of the smaller hotels didn't serve breakfast, so Lorenzo filled that gap. Café Aroma had its place in the local market.

As soon as I walked in, Lorenzo came straight to me.

"The delivery guy isn't coming today. Ty is loading the van. You'll do the deliveries. The urgent one is Aspen Lodge. I'll text you the details."

With the keys in hand, I turned right back around into the cold. Ty shut the van doors, waved, and walked inside. I checked Lorenzo's message, entered the lodge address into the GPS, and got moving.

After almost getting stuck in snow at an intersection, I finally parked in front of the stone-and-wood lodge. I carried the two boxes of donuts and muffins inside first, leaving them in the room the sleepy receptionist pointed to. Then I returned for the thermal boxes of coffee and hot chocolate and delivered them to the meeting room.

Before heading out, I stopped by the washroom to wipe sugar off my coat sleeve. When I stepped back into the hallway, I nearly stumbled over a big dog.

My whole heart melted. I knelt down and hugged the caramel Labrador around the neck. I missed the smell of animals. Loved their warmth. Reading animals had always come naturally to me long before vet school. The lab was friendly and licked my face.

"Are you lost?" I asked, leaning in to read his name tag.

He gave a short bark in response.

Just then, the door in front of me opened, and a dark-haired man in winter sports clothes stepped out. I stood up, caught off guard by eyes that seemed to take everything in around him.

"He yours?"

"No," he said with a lazy smile and a yawn. "I heard the bark and came to check."

I nodded. The dog barked again, took a few steps down the hall, looked back at me, barked once more, then sat, alert and waiting.

"I think he's trying to say something," the tall, lean man said.

I walked to the dog and crouched again. "What is it?"

The man watched us closely, clearly amused by the Beauty and the Beast moment, though I didn't think of myself as much of a beauty.

The lab trotted halfway down the hall, looked at me, and barked again. So I followed him.

And the man followed me.

A blast of cold air hit my face as we rounded the corner of the hallway. The dog vanished from sight, but I spotted a side door standing open. I hurried outside. The man came too.

An older gentleman with a cane was brushing snow off his pants. His beard and hair were white as snow, and his blue eyes were gentle. The dog circled him, barking.

"Archie, good boy!"

The lab licked his hand.

"Need help?" the man beside me asked, holding the elderly man's arm.

"I'm all right now. I slipped on the ice, and Archie went in to get help. He worries about me." He chuckled, rubbing the dog's head.

The stranger and I guided the elderly gentleman to his room on the second floor. He thanked us more than once, insisted he'd be fine, and closed the door, leaving the two of us alone in the quiet hallway. On the other side, Archie let out one last proud bark, like he was signing off his rescue mission.

"So... you talk to dogs?" the man asked, still wearing that just-woke-up smile, complete with pillow creases on his cheek.

"I have a connection with them," I said, heading toward the stairs.

"Them? Meaning... other animals too?"

He followed me down.

"Yes."

He waited for more, but I didn't elaborate. I was behind schedule now and didn't need more gum stuck to my boot. I hurried down the stairs, turned enough to wave at him, and rushed outside.

In the rearview mirror of the van, I saw him come out of the lodge and wave with arm stretched high in the cold air.

I pressed the gas and turned the corner.

3. A Love Story

What truly belongs to the heart always finds its way back.

My parents weren't perfect. Lorenzo and I liked to say that the older they got, the more they nitpicked each other. It was affectionate bickering—routine, predictable, but the kind that came only after years of showing up for the same person. They took their wedding vows seriously. They'd survived poverty, illness, and every "for better or worse" clause, even if some of those chapters were completed with heavy sighs and a few slammed doors. Now, they were finally able to enjoy the rewards of decades of work and sacrifice.

Last year, my dad started showing the first signs of Parkinson's. It was subtle at first, with just a tremor you might blame on fatigue. But my mom didn't ignore it. Within weeks, she had them both packed and relocated to a warmer climate. She spent hours online researching treatments, exercises, support groups and anything that might give him a better quality of life. Watching her step into that role made me admire her even more. That was the kind of love they built: steady, practical, loyal.

My mom loved telling me how they met as teenagers. Different towns, a mutual friend, and one brief afternoon together that changed everything. With no internet or cell phones, they relied on letters—pages filled with teenage sincerity and feelings that surprised them in their intensity.

Distance didn't intimidate them. My dad found ways to visit whenever he could, even if it meant racing from school to the bus stop, arriving sweaty and out of breath for fifteen stolen minutes before he had to turn around and head back home. The relationship was innocent, but the attachment was real. He wrote her poems, and she kept them locked in a small wooden box like they were gold.

When my mom turned sixteen, my grandparents moved even farther. She sent my dad her new address and more letters, but they never reached him. She wrote two more and got silence in return. She thought he'd changed his mind. What she didn't know was that his family had moved too after his parents divorced. My dad even made the trip to her old town once, asking around, but no one seemed interested in helping with information. Distance and silence weren't kind to lovestruck teenagers.

Four years passed. They missed each other, but life kept moving. My mom dated someone for a while, but she couldn't shake the feeling that she was pretending. She cried over my dad more than she cared to admit. And my dad dated a few girls, trying to recreate what he'd lost, but nothing fit. Both of them were living with a quiet ache they didn't talk about.

Then, one morning, as my mom was heading to college, my dad appeared on the corner of her street. She dropped her books and ran to him. He caught her and held on hard like a man who'd been searching forever and had finally found the one thing he couldn't lose again.

He told her he had never stopped looking. He'd followed every lead, every vague detail, until he found the right thread to pull. Today, with social media and search engines, that kind of persistence seems almost unnecessary. But back then, he had to rely on patience, luck, and sheer stubbornness. It worked. After that day, they never separated again.

My story, though, went the other way.

I got the kind of guy who believed proximity was a love language and had no concept of personal space. Someone who turned my life into a surveillance lesson. So I shut it all down: social media, email, every predictable pattern.

And yet, part of me still believed that if someone ever fell in love with me, he'd have to put in some effort to reach me. Not chase me. Not hunt me down. But show intention. Show he meant it.

P.F. had every technological advantage in the world to track me. He didn't do it because he valued me; he did it because he needed someone to fill a void he didn't know how to deal with. A mother-shaped vacancy. Unhealthy. Unfair. And certainly not love.

"I need you, Baby Sabrina," he would say.

Needed me for what?

If a man ever showed interest in me again, I wanted it to be because he wanted to know me. Because he wanted to stand beside me, not cling to me. Someone willing to walk with me through whatever valleys and mountains life had lined up.

Some days, I wonder if that was too much to hope for. Other days, I reminded myself that my parents managed to find each other twice, by chance and by choice.

Maybe that kind of love wasn't impossible. Just rare.

And rare things were worth waiting for.

4. An Unexpected Visit

Never underestimate a small gesture. Sometimes it holds more than you think.

"Whew. We really need to get more organized with these deliveries," I told Lorenzo as I slipped behind the counter at Café Aroma. He was at the register dealing with a rushed customer who darted out through the door, letting a blast of cold air sweep in.

"Today was an emergency, but orders have been piling up," he said, switching to a lively group of ski-jacketed friends. "We'll talk about it later. Go see if they need help in the kitchen."

I peeled off my heavy coat and hung it in the cramped little office (really just a corner beside the cleaning-supply closet with a makeshift sliding door.) I grabbed the dark green apron with the café logo, tightened my ponytail, and washed my hands at the sink next to the massive oven. The smells hit me all at once—cinnamon, fresh bread, strong coffee.

Four seasonal workers were hustling around the kitchen, two girls, two guys, students picking up holiday shifts. They all smiled when I walked in.

"What do you need help with?" I asked.

The short-haired girl pulled a tray of muffins out of the oven. "Can you check the soup? I think there are still some frozen chunks in there."

I glanced at the wall clock. Lunchtime crowds would be arriving any minute. I moved fast, hopping between tasks. From the kitchen doorway, I caught flashes of the café: round tables, colorful winter coats, people laughing over pastries.

I was on my way out with a tray of fresh bread when I saw him walk in and froze. It was the same man I'd seen at Aspen Lodge. Green jacket. Hard to miss. I stepped back immediately and handed the tray to one of the girls.

Hidden by the doorframe, I watched him approach Lorenzo. They exchanged a few words, then Lorenzo nodded, told one of the baristas to cover the register, and headed straight for the kitchen.

"Sabrina, there's a guy out there asking for you."

I grabbed Lorenzo by the sleeve and pulled him into the makeshift office. "Tell him I'm not here. I barely know him. We just bumped into each other at Aspen Lodge. We helped a man who slipped on the ice, that's all."

"He said it's important." Lorenzo gave me a worried look.

What could some random stranger possibly have to say that was so important? "Lorenzo, the last thing I need is another... situation in my life."

He sighed, went back out, talked to the guy, then returned and handed me my wallet.

I stared. I hadn't even realized it was missing. Usually I kept it in my coat pocket.

"He said you dropped it in the hallway at the lodge when you made the delivery. At least go thank him," Lorenzo said before heading back to the register.

The man was already pushing the glass door open to leave. Thank him for what? Anyone decent would return a wallet. Lorenzo shot me a look that said *go*. I let out a huff and hurried after the man without even grabbing my coat.

"Hey!" I called.

The cold hit me like a slap to my face. I hugged myself, my orange sweater doing absolutely nothing to keep out the wind.

He turned, smiled, and walked back toward me. I thanked him quickly and was about to retreat into the warm café when he said:

"Oh, good. I was hoping to catch you."

"What do you mean?" I rubbed my arms to keep warm.

"Larry, Archie's owner, asked me to thank you for what you did. And he wanted you to have this." He pulled a small envelope from the pocket of his green jacket. "He told me to deliver it to you personally."

By then I was shivering so hard my teeth rattled. I reached for the envelope, fumbled it, and dropped it into the thin layer of snow. We both crouched at the same time and bumped heads hard. Pain shot through my skull, and I lost my balance, falling straight onto the icy sidewalk.

I wasn't sure what hurt more, the cold or the impact.

The man grabbed my arm to steady me and helped me stand. I was still dazed, so when he guided me back into the café, I didn't argue. He pulled out a chair and I sank into it, pressing my hand against the lump forming on my forehead.

He said something. My ears were ringing. He went to the counter and returned with a steaming mug of tea. I thanked him.

"Hurting a lot?" he asked as he sat across from me.

"Getting better." I sipped the tea, letting the warmth seep back into my body. I glanced at Lorenzo at the register. He gave me a weird look, some mix of amusement and concern.

"The envelope!" I said, eyes wide.

The man set it on the table and nudged it toward me. "Better open it."

I raised my eyebrows. Who opens something personal in front of a stranger? "I'll read it later."

"Noah."

"What?"

"My name. It's Noah, Sabrina." He smiled.

Oh. The wallet. Of course he knew my name. I slipped the envelope into my pocket and stoop up, still holding the mug. "Right. Well, I should get back to work."

Noah stood too. He pulled a business card from his pocket and handed it to me. I took it, confused.

"If you need to talk after you read Larry's note, that's my contact." He gave a small wave and left.

Why on earth would I need to talk to him after reading a card from a man I barely knew?

Maybe the bump on my head was worse than I thought because my encounter with Noah didn't make any sense.

5. The Card

Sometimes the surprising things start with something completely ordinary.

I scrubbed my damp hair with the towel, trying to get rid of the last traces of the day. I liked the smell of coffee, but not enough to spend an entire shift smelling like a human espresso. The long shower washed the scent off me, but not the exhaustion of being on my feet all day. As a vet, I was used to walking nonstop, but outdoors, not trapped inside four walls. Still, I needed the job, and Lorenzo needed the help.

I sat on the bed and pulled Larry's envelope onto my lap. Noah had handed it to me only a few hours earlier. I adjusted my robe and leaned back against the pillows. Stretching my legs felt like heaven.

I slid out the small white card. Larry's handwriting shook across the page:

My dear, thank you for rescuing me this morning. Archie clearly knew who to call. These little Christmas miracles keep me going.

As a token of thanks, I'd like to invite you to dinner tomorrow at the address below. I also took the liberty of inviting the kind Noah.

Make an old man feel some joy this Christmas. — Larry

I read it twice. Then again. I considered my options: ignore it, come up with an excuse. Accepting wasn't even on the table. Why would I have dinner with two complete strangers?

I set the card on the nightstand and went to dry my hair.

When Lorenzo got home, he immediately brought up Noah. I gave him the short version of the head-bumping fiasco. I didn't mention Larry's note. If I did, Lorenzo would insist it was my civic Christmas duty to go.

He disappeared into his room while I heated up canned soup. Later, he reappeared in pajamas, filled a bowl, and sat with me at the small table. Outside, snow drifted down in slow, weightless flakes.

"So," he said, spoon in hand, "what exactly did you and Noah talk about?"

"I told you. Nothing important."

"I saw him give you an envelope."

He didn't miss a thing. "It was just a thank-you card from the man we helped at the lodge."

Lorenzo scraped the spoon around the bowl. "Your tone says otherwise."

"You're nosy," I muttered. My brother read me better than anyone—my voice, my posture, the tiny things and gestures I never noticed.

"You interlace your fingers when you're anxious," he added. "Like you're doing right now."

I unclasped my hands and placed them in my lap. "It was a long day."

"Okay. If you don't want to talk…" He stood up with his empty bowl and walked to the sink. I watched him from behind the counter that separated the small kitchen from the living area.

"Larry, that older gentleman, invited me to dinner tomorrow," I finally said.

Lorenzo turned, leaned against the counter, and folded his arms. "And?"

"I don't know…"

"Why not? It's a nice Christmas gesture."

I snorted. Predictable. "You mean, Christmas ambush. He invited Noah too."

Lorenzo raised an eyebrow and smiled. "Interesting."

I stood up with my bowl. "Interesting? Try awkward."

"I've given my opinion. What time is the dinner?"

"He wrote six. But that's peak time at the café." I doubted Lorenzo would let me abandon him during rush hour.

"I'll manage. You should go," he said, way too easily. My expression must have shown my confusion, because he added, "I'll tweak the schedule. The students always want extra shifts anyway."

With no real argument left, I agreed. But something in my gut told me this wasn't going to be a normal dinner.

6. The Dinner

The baggage people carry is always full of surprises.

I parked my SUV along the snow-packed curb. Larry's card sat on the passenger seat, and I checked the address again before glancing out the window. It matched the GPS. And the little house beside me, straight out of a storybook, was exactly where Larry had invited me.

The warm glow from the streetlamp made the place look like a Christmas card illustration. A life-size nativity scene sat in the middle of the yard, buried in soft snow. The roof and both front windows were trimmed with blue lights, flickering against the night.

I looked down at my red wool coat and almost laughed. Add the white knit hat, and I basically looked like Mrs. Claus showing up for her shift.

I stepped out of the car, and before I could reach the doorbell, the door swung open and Archie bounded straight toward me.

"Good boy," I said as I crouched, getting a face full of enthusiastic dog kisses.

Larry stood at the door with his arms open like a grandfather welcoming his granddaughter. His red-and-green sweater and bright white hair didn't help. There was Santa right in front of me. For reasons I couldn't fully explain, I hurried into his arms and hugged him. It felt familiar, comforting in the same way hugging my grandfathers used to feel.

"Come in, come in, Sabrina. Too cold out there," he said, closing the door behind us.

The living room was small and warm, the kind of cozy that hit you all at once. The fireplace glowed in the corner, decked out in Christmas decorations and giving off a steady, soothing heat.

I realized I was curious about Larry. Did he live alone? What was he doing at Aspen Lodge in a room, since he had his own home in the village? A slight tremor in his hands caught my eye as he gestured for me to sit on the plaid sofa. Archie followed me and curled up at my feet.

"Thank you for the invitation," I said. I'd come mostly because Lorenzo pushed me into it but a small part of me felt like I was supposed to be here.

Larry chuckled. "Not many young people say yes to dinner with an old man, especially this time of year."

Ouch. Guilty. I started to mumble something, but the doorbell cut me off. Archie raced ahead as Larry went to open it.

Noah stepped inside holding a gift box. I immediately regretted showing up empty-handed.

The men exchanged greetings, and Larry thanked him for the present, placing it on the coffee table. Noah shrugged off his black jacket, then turned to me.

"Hey, Sabrina. Good to see you again." His hand was warm when he shook mine, warmer than I expected for someone who'd just come in from the cold.

He offered to take my coat, and I stood to unbutton the heavy thing. He hung it neatly on a coat rack. He sat down at the other end of the sofa where I was.

Archie returned to his spot by my feet as Larry repeated what he'd told me earlier.

"Thank you, Noah, for accepting an invitation from an old man."

Noah rested his hands on his knees and smiled. "My pleasure. This time of year always makes you think about what really matters. And a dinner like this, it's a gift."

I had to fight the urge to make a face. Was he actually that sincere, or was this some kind of performance? Regardless, I nodded along like I agreed then mentally called myself out. Who was acting now?

We made small talk about Christmas, the cold, and the ski village. Nothing personal, just preferences about winter food and activities. A soft *ding* from down the hall made Larry stand up, and Archie sprang up with him.

"The oven calls," he said, disappearing through a door.

Minutes later, the smell of roasted turkey began filling the house.

"And your head?" Noah asked, motioning to my forehead.

I touched the spot. The bump had nearly vanished. "Oh, fine. I barely feel it now."

"I'm glad you came. Larry seems... like a good man. He looks..." Noah smiled as he looked around the living room.

"Looks like Santa?" I offered.

"That too. But there's something else. In his eyes." Noah stared into the fireplace flames, his expression distant for a moment.

Larry returned and invited us to the dining room. The table looked ready for the front cover of a Christmas magazine—festive but simple.

That's when I noticed the cabinet behind him. Its entire top was covered in framed photos. Most of them were of the same woman at different ages—short hair that went from dark to gray, bright eyes, red lipstick, always smiling softly.

I sat where Larry pointed, across from Noah. Larry settled at the head of the table, facing the photographs.

"Agnes," he said.

I looked at him and blinked hard.

"My wife. We were married fifty-three years. She passed away five years ago. My Christmases haven't been the same. My life hasn't been the same." He seemed to drift into the words. "On our anniversary, I always go to Aspen Lodge. We used to celebrate there."

A lump formed in my throat. Fifty-three years with someone. And then losing them. I didn't know what to say, so I focused on the table instead. The smell of roasted turkey drifted over everything, grounding me.

I reached for a serving spoon just to keep my hands busy. Noah did the same. We filled our plates with turkey that Larry had carved, mashed potatoes, cranberry sauce.

"Tell us about Agnes," Noah said.

Larry did. For the entire meal.

He told us about living in different towns before the wedding, how their relationship was always interrupted by distance, how they never had children but supported hundreds of foster kids. His eyes brimmed with tears often, yet he smiled through every story. When the emotions swelled, his hands trembled slightly more.

Noah listened closely, asking gentle questions. Everything went a little quieter, like we all felt the weight of his memories.

If I'd arrived at this dinner reluctantly, by the end of the night I knew there was nowhere else I was supposed to be. This little storybook house wasn't just charming—it had a real history, a real ache, a real love inside it. I didn't want the evening to end.

When Larry spoke about Agnes's last days, how cancer took her, I stared at the photos and swallowed hard. My nose prickled. Noah must have noticed something about it, because he tapped his own nose and pointed discreetly at the napkins.

Heat crawled up my neck. Great. Runny nose. I dabbed it quickly with a napkin while Larry described her funeral. When he excused himself and stepped into the kitchen, I took my chance and hurried to the small bathroom off the dining room. Just as I feared, my nose was a mess. I washed my face, blew my nose, and dried everything with a handful of tissues. I made it back before Larry returned.

I gave Noah an embarrassed half-smile. He just smiled back.

"What a story," he said.

"Tell me about it. I'm useless with emotional stuff," I admitted, rubbing the corners of my eyes.

"Agnes must've been something special. But when we look at someone through love, we tend to see the best in them."

"Probably true," I said, sniffling lightly.

Larry returned with a beautiful apple pie. He told us Agnes had taught him to cook and claimed she used to say the student had surpassed the teacher. Judging by the pie and the cinnamon tea he brewed she wasn't wrong.

I wished the night could go on longer, but once we finished cleaning up, I noticed how tired Larry looked. Noah and I said our goodbyes and stepped into the cold night. With the soft snow coming down and the street quiet, he opened the SUV door and didn't move until I was seated. I waved and pulled onto the snow-covered street. A glance in the rearview showed him still there, standing in the dark with one hand in his pocket and a quiet, lingering wave.

Later, in the comfort of my bed, I replayed the entire night. A strange, soft nostalgia washed over me like I was missing something I couldn't name.

7. Out of Focus

In such a short time, he had already become essential to my growth.

In the days after dinner at Larry's house, I felt like I was walking through a movie shot slightly out of focus. My life looked the same on the outside, living with my brother, working shifts at the café, but something inside me felt... off. As if I'd stepped into a life that didn't quite fit, like wearing someone else's coat. I couldn't explain it. A strange ache for something that wasn't mine, for a life that didn't belong to me.

I hadn't seen Larry again. The day after the dinner, I stopped by his house with a small gift and a thank-you card. He didn't answer the door. I tucked the wrapped package into his mailbox and lingered for a moment in front of the nativity scene. The snow was falling gently, settling on Mary's blue robe and the wise men's crowns. I whispered a prayer I couldn't even understand. I trusted God could.

Noah had vanished too. I knew nothing about him except his first name and the warmth of his handshake. He didn't seem to live in the village, at least not permanently. He'd looked like a guest at Aspen Lodge. Maybe he'd already packed up and left for the city.

Funny how a chance meeting followed by a dinner I hadn't even wanted to attend could leave such an unexpected emptiness behind. Was my life so busy, so mechanical, that I never slowed down enough to notice the weight of simple moments? I'd never been the contemplative type. Stopping for no reason felt pointless to me whether it was watching snow fall on rooftops or people walking down the street. Maybe that was a kind of pride, thinking I always had something more important to do. Larry, with all his years and quiet wisdom, had learned the opposite. Meanwhile, I was still in life's kindergarten.

Lorenzo noticed something was off. He always did. Whenever we were home, I sat with my fingers laced together, my telltale anxiety pose. My situation was unusual, I tried to tell myself. A vet working in a café, living with her brother, with no idea what the next year would look like. But the truth was simpler: I wanted to see Larry again. I wanted to hear more of his story.

At the end of the week, while delivering breakfast to Aspen Lodge, I caught a glimpse of Noah getting into a car. He didn't see me. For half a second, I considered honking, waving, anything to get his attention. I didn't. Watching him stirred the same feeling I had felt in Larry's house.

I told myself I could just go back to Larry's house another day. No big deal.

On Saturday, Lorenzo gave me the full day off, so I decided
to ski. I wasn't great at it, but I managed fine on the interme-
diate slope. The resort was packed, kids wobbling down the
hill, adults showing off their turns, a few people rolling in the
snow after spectacular wipeouts. On my last ride up the lift, skis
dangling above the pine trees and the cold air cutting through
the parts of my face my scarf didn't reach, I made up my mind:
I would visit Larry again.

I didn't have his phone number. Actually, I hadn't even seen
him with a cell phone. The only number I had was Noah's,
written on the card I'd tossed into my nightstand drawer. Calling him for Larry's information felt pointless. He probably
knew as little as I did.

That strange feeling stayed with me after a hot shower and
dinner. It only grew stronger when I stopped by a little gift shop
on Main Street and bought a soft scarf for Larry. Red, of course.
My heart was thudding the whole drive to his house. What if he
wasn't home?

When I pulled up to the curb, I saw a woman in a bathrobe
and boots step out of the house next door. She walked toward
me in the snow. The expression on her face told me everything
before she even spoke.

Larry was in the hospital.

My stomach flipped. She didn't have many details, only that
an ambulance had taken him several days earlier. The day after
our dinner. Archie was fine, she added quickly, he'd been staying
with her and entertaining her grandkids.

I thanked her, stunned, and hurried back home. My hands shook as I rummaged through my nightstand drawer until I found Noah's business card. Without giving myself more time to panic, I called him.

Within the hour, we were at the hospital together. And the entire drive there, my heart hammered like it was bracing for a loss I wasn't ready to face.

8. Refocusing

What if my whole life had been standing on unstable ground?

There are only a handful of moments that make us stop and reconsider the life we're living. The fear of losing someone or losing our own life usually tops the list.

Noah and I didn't get tragic news from the nurse, but we didn't get comforting news either. Larry had suffered a heart attack.

According to the nurse, he'd already gone through a life-saving procedure and was recovering, but he wasn't out of the woods. She pointed us toward the recovery ward, and we followed her directions through a maze of curtains dividing the beds. We found his number printed on a small card clipped above the curtain.

Before we could step inside, a voice behind us said:

"Are you relatives of Mr. Larry Smith?"

Noah and I turned around. A young brunette with sharp, observing eyes stood there holding a clipboard. She introduced herself as Amy Ho, one of the hospital's social workers.

"No, we're friends," Noah said, and introduced us both.

Amy nodded, flipped through the papers on her clipboard, and asked, "Do either of you know if he has any family nearby?"

We explained that he was a widower and had no children.

Amy let out a quiet breath. "Mr. Smith will be released to-morrow, but he can't stay alone. I've arranged a caregiver, but only for two hours a day. He'll need someone with him, some-one who can stay overnight for the first few weeks. Parkinson's often worsens after something like this."

Parkinson's.

My stomach clenched. The tremor in Larry's hands had been just like my father's.

"I can spend a few nights with him," I heard myself say. It came out fast, almost impulsive. Only later did it hit me that I had no idea how I'd balance work at the café and caring for Larry.

"Count me in too," Noah added.

Amy took down our phone numbers, made a few notes, and told us she'd check in after we saw him. Then she disappeared down the hallway.

Noah and I pulled back the curtain. The space was plain and tidy, lit by a single overhead lamp. A soft beep from a nearby monitor broke the quiet, and the faint smell of sanitizer lin-gered.

Larry was sleeping. For a moment, all I could do was take him in. His white hair, usually soft and fluffed like fresh snow, was flattened against his head. His beard had grown unevenly. His hands rested on the blanket, shaking slightly with each breath. The staff was doing their best, but small comforts weren't top priority in any hospital.

I glanced at Noah. He gave me a quiet, understanding look.

Larry stirred and slowly opened his eyes. The tiredness made the wrinkles around them deeper. The moment he spotted us, he smiled and lifted his shaky hand.

"What a good surprise to see you two," he said, voice thin but warm.

We exchanged a few gentle words. I reassured him that Archie was safe with the neighbor. Larry closed his eyes in relief.

I pulled a chair closer to the bed and sat down, Noah by my side, still standing. "We talked to the social worker," I said softly. "She wants someone with you for the first few nights."

Larry opened his eyes again, a faint crease of worry between his brows. "I don't want to be a burden."

"You're not," I told him. "I can stay with you until you feel a bit better."

He let out a breath, the kind that came from someone who hadn't felt cared for in a while. "That's kind of you, my dear. I don't like the idea of going back to an empty house."

"You won't be alone," I said.

Before we left, Noah rested a hand lightly on the metal railing of the bed. "Don't worry about a thing," he told Larry. "I'll pick you up tomorrow and take you home. Sabrina and I will make sure you're settled."

Larry's eyes softened. "I'm lucky to have you both."

Noah gave a small nod. "We've got you, Larry."

We confirmed everything with Amy, who jotted down the plan. In the hospital lobby, with patients bundled in coats waiting for their turn to get help, I turned to Noah.

"I'll stay with him for the first few nights," I said.

"My schedule's flexible during the day," he replied. "I can stop by to check on him. And you have my number. Call me anytime."

It occurred to me that he hadn't asked for my number. Considering the circumstances, it made more sense that he should have it. I couldn't hide from everyone forever, not because of P.F. My new phone had barely any contacts: family, Marsha from the equestrian center, a few contacts related to the café.

So I gave my number to Noah. Oddly, it didn't feel uncomfortable. We didn't really know each other, but we had Larry in common. And right now, he needed both of us.

We said goodnight, and I drove home to tell Lorenzo what had happened.

He listened carefully, then nodded. "I'm glad, Sabrina. You're starting to open up again. We'll adjust your schedule so you have time for Larry. And I want to meet him, by the way."

Wrapped in a quilt on the couch, I sighed. "It must be hard to be alone. Larry was married for fifty-three years. Think about that. Now it's just him and a dog."

Lorenzo leaned back in the lazy chair opposite me and exhaled. "But you and Noah stepped up. That matters."

He was right.

That day shifted something in me with the news about Larry, the hospital visit, and the partnership with Noah . It made me rethink a lot of the plans I'd been gripping so tightly. Maybe shutting everyone out wasn't safety. Maybe it was just fear.

I snuggled under the quilt. "Today was... different."

Lorenzo frowned. "Because of Larry?"

"Yeah. And Noah. And—me, I guess." I sat up and pulled my hair back. "I've been living like someone who's expecting the worst."

"Sab, you've been through enough. But you're allowed to step out of survival mode."

I let out a breath. "It scares me."

"Good," Lorenzo said with a smirk. "Means you're not made of ice and snow."

I rolled my eyes, but he wasn't wrong. Maybe protecting myself had turned into isolation. And maybe it was time to do something else.

I depended on people. And people depended on me.

What I didn't know yet was that this new focus, this new willingness to step into someone else's life, would bring me more joy than I expected.

And it would become one more chapter leading me toward the best version of my story.

9. Philosophy

Nothing disarms us like being treated with respect.

As we had planned, Noah brought Larry home the next afternoon. I packed a small overnight bag and headed there before dinner. Larry looked brighter than he had at the hospital, freshly showered thanks to Noah.

I made a simple meal of scrambled eggs, toast and steamed broccoli, and we ate at the small kitchen table with Archie wedged between our legs, waiting for food to magically fall from the table. I saw Larry the way you'd see a grandfather. But Noah? Maybe a cousin at best, a distant one, the kind you meet once every ten years in grandparents' funerals. Calling him a friend felt like a stretch. I still knew very little about him, and that bothered me more than I wanted to admit. Asking him outright seemed like giving too much of myself away, too soon.

We kept the conversation around Larry's hospital stay, but it wasn't heavy or sad. Larry saw life through a lens most people didn't. Death, he said, didn't frighten him; it was simply part of the deal. Something we all knew but pretend not to think about.

"I don't buy green bananas anymore," Larry said with a straight face. "Chances are I won't be around to see them ripen."

I burst out laughing. Noah shook his head, amused.

Larry's funny musings about death continued for some time, with one comment more unexpected than the last. Noah and I laughed while making our own attempt to throw in our own jokes, though none of them were nearly as funny.

After dinner, Noah took over the kitchen, washing dishes, wiping counters, while I sat with Larry in the living room. Christmas music drifted softly through the house. I'd left a small gift in his mailbox the day he went to the hospital, and he opened it now. He smiled as he pulled out the scarf from the box and told me Noah had given him a toque in the exact same style. I was glad.

We grew quiet, listening to the old CD player humming out *Silent Night*. Archie curled at Larry's feet, loyal as ever. Larry blinked slowly, fighting sleep, his mug slipping a little in his hand.

"It's been a long day," I said. "You should get to bed."

He nodded. I took his cup before it tipped, and he thanked me again for staying the night. As I turned off the stereo, I heard him exchanging a few words with Noah in the kitchen before shuffling down the hallway and closing his bedroom door.

When I reached the kitchen, Noah was drying the last pan.

"He tired out fast," I said, rinsing out our leftover cups.

Noah leaned against the counter and shook the water from his hands. "Heart surgery takes more out of a person than we think."

I wanted to ask Noah about his parents and siblings, whether he lived near them, but I didn't even know where he himself lived. The gap in information felt strange now.

Noah hung the towel on a hook. "I should get going. If you need anything in the night, call me. I sleep light."

I usually slept like a rock. But tonight I knew I'd be awake for a while, partly worrying about Larry, partly... curious. There was something about Noah I wanted to understand. All I knew was what I'd seen in these past few days: he was thoughtful, steady, discreet.

We walked to the door together, and my tongue practically itched with questions. But if he wasn't offering anything personal, maybe he wasn't ready to.

"I never thanked you," I said. "For... building this bridge between me and Larry."

The words sounded clunky coming out, but they were honest.

Noah slipped on his coat and turned toward me. "I always thought you were the bridge. If you hadn't helped Larry at the lodge, I wouldn't have met him at all."

"He's a special man."

"He is," Noah agreed quietly.

We stood at the door for a moment, neither of us moving.

"Will you sleep okay?" he asked.

"Hope so. I'm going to make another cup of tea and try to relax."

He hesitated, then put his coat back on the hook. "Want company for that tea?"

My heart did a quick, embarrassing little hop. Not the swoony kind you read in paperbacks, just a warm jolt under my ribs, a sudden flush in my cheeks.

I nodded.

A few minutes later, we were sitting across from each other at the kitchen table once more that night, chamomile tea steaming between us. We ended up talking for almost two hours, not about our personal histories, but about life, purpose, faith, timing. The big human things. And on those, we thought almost exactly alike. It felt less like small talk and more like... alignment.

Maybe it was the season. Maybe it was the soft glow of Larry's fairy-tale house. Maybe it was the white-haired man sleeping down the hall. Whatever it was, when Noah finally said goodnight, I felt lighter like the snow that had started falling again outside.

I slept in the guest bedroom. When I woke up the next morning, for a second I wondered if I'd imagined the whole evening. But then I walked into the kitchen. The teacups I'd left drying weren't there. The chamomile box Noah set on the table was gone. No little note. No message on my phone. Nothing.

Part of me had hoped for something, for a sign of my time with Noah at the table. I tried not to think too much of it.

I helped Larry with his morning routine, made his breakfast, and got ready for work. Lorenzo was being patient with my schedule, but he needed me. I was halfway out the door when Larry said Noah would stop by within the hour.

A very real, strong temptation washed over me not to leave. To stay and cross paths with Noah. But duty won. So I stepped back into the cold morning, through the snow-covered streets, and headed to the café.

10. Another Stalker

The greatest shame is being accused of what you despise most.

My eyes burned with sleep as I served a line of hungry, chatty customers. An elderly couple stood at the counter debating at length whether they wanted the chocolate muffin or the blueberry one, latte or Americano, butter or cream cheese. The line behind them stretched all the way to the door. Every time I suggested something, they changed their minds. It was like negotiating a peace treaty over baked goods.

They finally made a decision, and the line moved faster. At the register, Lorenzo threw me worried glances every few minutes. When the café finally emptied a bit, he leaned toward me.

"Want to go home and take a nap?" he asked.

"No, no. Just give me one strong coffee and I'll survive," I said, closing the glass case full of blueberry muffins, almond croissants, maple walnut scones and more.

"I need to run to the bank. I'll ask Maggie to help out. The kitchen rush should be over by now."

Maggie, a plus-size young woman with dimples that looked like Gilmore Girls' Sookie, took over, and Lorenzo left. For a while, the café stayed nearly empty with just a couple customers buying drinks to go. I grabbed a broom and started sweeping the floor, gathering crumbs into the dustpan. Then I stepped outside to sweep the entryway. A gravel truck had just passed, scattering pebbles across the wet concrete.

The striped blue-and-white awning kept most of the snow off, but the boots of winter tourists dragged in all sorts of slush and dirt as well. The cold had eased some, so even with just a sweater and the green apron, I felt comfortable enough. It was nice to get a break from the constant smell of coffee.

Cars splashed through the slushy street, sending dirty snow to the curb. People drifted along the sidewalks, shopping for Christmas gifts. The decorations—greens and reds wrapped around the street lamps—broke up the otherwise endless white of winter.

I made a mental note to buy something for Lorenzo. And for Larry. I wasn't sure about Noah. Did one buy gifts for... whatever Noah was? I opened the glass door to step back inside, and that was when I saw Noah, crossing the street a little farther up. And curiosity, that treacherous mouse nibbling inside my brain, went wild. I dropped the broom inside the café and waved quickly at Maggie.

"Be right back!" I mouthed.

She blinked at me, confused, and I slipped out.

And then... I did it. I followed him.

Full-on, no-shame, undercover-mission followed him.

I crept behind street poles and Christmas-decorated bushes playing sleuth. My common sense whispered that this was ridiculous, that I could simply ask the man a question like a normal human being. But common sense had taken the afternoon off.

Noah walked into a souvenir shop. Inside, there was a cheerful explosion of overpriced trinkets: maple-leaf magnets, miniature ski sets, flannel blankets folded like they were auditioning for a catalog. A rotating rack of postcards spun every time someone touched it. I watched Noah browse as if choosing between keychains was a life-or-death decision. I got closer and pretended to talk on my phone, leaning casually against a lamppost. People passed without noticing me.

Minutes later, Noah came out with a small green-and-red paper bag. He kept walking, and so did I. He greeted a group of two men and a woman, chatted for a minute, and kept going.

Then he stopped. Abruptly.

And turned.

My soul left my body like in those cartoons of the past. Through my mouth. I dove behind a parked black van like someone avoiding laser beams. I inhaled my soul back, heart pounding.

A rush of pure, undiluted embarrassment shot up my neck and burned my cheeks. What was I doing?

I didn't even know what I hoped to find out during my investigation.

Before I could regroup, a car drove too close to the curb and splashed a tidal wave of icy slush right at me. I shrieked as freezing dirty water soaked my jeans halfway to the knee.

Perfect. Just perfect.

Noah disappeared into the crowd, and I stood there dripping like a snowman in early spring. I spun around, ready to slink back to the café, and slammed right into someone.

"Sabrina!"

Lorenzo's face appeared in front of me, alarmed. "What happened to you?"

"I was... well... I was standing there, and a car came by, and... it threw all this slush on me—"

He stared at me like he was waiting for the real story. "You're bright red. Where's your coat?"

"I... ugh." I was cold, wet, and humiliated. Full combo number three on the embarrassment menu, the daily special.

Lorenzo wrapped an arm around my shoulders and steered me back toward the café. I rushed into the bathroom to clean up and used half a roll of paper towels trying to dry my jeans. They were still wet and muddy, but at least I didn't squish when I walked.

I stepped into Lorenzo's tiny office. He leaned back in his rolling chair, giving me a look that said *you're not getting away without explaining*.

"So?" he asked.

I gave the smile of a cat caught with a canary in its mouth. "I was... watching Noah."

His eyebrow shot up. "Watching? Watching what, exactly?"

"He walked by and... I kind of... went after him."

"You *followed* him?" His voice jumped an octave.

I nodded.

"Why, Sabrina?"

I twisted my apron in my hands. "I was curious."

"About what?"

"I don't know where he lives, what he does, where he's from."

Lorenzo stared at me. "So you decided to stalk him? Really?"

The word hit me right in the pride. I, of all people, being accused of that.

"I wasn't stalking!" I snapped. "I was... observing."

"Behind a van? Without a coat? While getting sprayed by street sludge?"

I pressed my lips together. "It sounds worse when you say it."

He came around the desk and put a hand on my arm.

"I'm sorry. That was harsh. But why don't you just ask him? Talk to him. Instead of freezing in the street like a penguin with a secret agenda?"

I sighed long, defeated. "I don't want to get too close. I'm leaving soon. No point starting something."

"Sabrina, this mystery world you've built in your head, none of it makes sense. It doesn't hurt to make friends, even if you're not staying forever."

Maybe he was right. Or maybe I was just tired.

"I need a shower," I muttered. "I'll run home and come back."

Lorenzo kissed my forehead. "Rest. Come back when the late-afternoon rush hits. Maggie and I can manage for now."

I grabbed my bag and headed out. What I didn't expect was to step onto the sidewalk—cold jeans, bruised pride, damp dignity—and almost collide straight into Noah.

11. The Invitation

Why commit a single blunder when I can upgrade to the deluxe package at no extra cost?

I pushed open the café's glass door, bells dinging, and stepped outside, shoving my arms into my coat sleeves as a blast of winter air slapped me awake. I lowered my head to zip up the front and—ow!—crashed straight into something solid. No, someone.

Noah. Perfect.

I immediately lost my balance. My right foot landed on a floating chunk of ice in a half-frozen puddle. For a full second, I swear I saw myself falling in slow motion—arms flailing, mouth open—an Olympic-level slapstick disaster.

But Noah caught me. Both hands wrapped around my arms, steady, warm, preventing the kind of fall that would've ended with me face-first on the pavement or, worse, trending on

TikTok. I straightened up, trying to retrieve at least a shred of dignity.

"Thanks," I muttered, not quite brave enough to meet his eyes yet.

Then I felt him looking me over as if assessing the damage. Or maybe just confirming it. Because the truth was unavoidable: I looked awful. Hair a mess, eyelids swollen with sleep, coat stained with coffee. And my scent... let's just say it wasn't a fragrance sold in stores. A mix of coffee and... well... yesterday's shower.

Noah's expression shifted from relaxed to concerned in a flash.

"Sorry I couldn't move out of the way fast enough. Where are you rushing to? Did something happen with Larry?"

I ran my fingers through the sad excuse of a ponytail on top of my head. "No. I was just heading home."

"You look... you look..." He gave me another full-body scan, gentler this time. "Busy day, huh?"

I thumbed over my shoulder toward the café. "Lots of work."

He held two cute, glittery Christmas paper bags and said, very casually:

"Why don't you take the night off? I'll stay with Larry."

I considered it for a few long moments. Maybe even an eternity. Had my brain stopped working? I was tired. Frustrated. Anxious. An emotional pressure cooker. I desperately needed rest, silence, space to reassess my completely ridiculous behavior.

"All right," I said, exhaling without realizing I'd been holding my breath. "Tomorrow morning I'll stop by and check if you need anything."

"Keep me posted."

"Keep me posted." I repeated his words automatically, though my brain wanted to say something entirely different. Several things, really. None of them appropriate for someone in my messy state. I needed a shower before I could say anything else.

He raised his hand in a simple, charming wave and continued walking. I finally zipped my coat and took a few steps... then froze.

I was a mature woman, right? Responsible, dependable, professional. So why couldn't I at least ask where Noah lived? I inhaled, ready to turn back, but didn't need to.

"Sabrina!"

I spun around so fast I nearly slipped again. My rebellious heart leapt like it had been waiting for exactly this moment since my arrival at Whistler.

"What is it?" If I sounded rude, you can blame my nervous system, not me.

Noah hesitated like someone about to jump off a cliff into glacial water.

"I was wondering if... some time... we could grab a coffee."

My mouth opened. Closed. Opened again.

He kept talking, stumbling over the words in the most charming way:

"I mean, you work in a café, so maybe you're sick of coffee. It could be tea. Or hot chocolate. And it doesn't have to be there, of course. Somewhere else. If you want. What do you think?"

For a moment, everything around us looked like a movie scene: distant traffic noise, people carrying Christmas bags, twinkle lights overhead, a dog dressed as a reindeer crossing the street like it was the most normal thing in the world. And me—messy, tired, smelling like day-old espresso—feeling something I had never felt before.

It wasn't butterflies in my stomach. More like standing on one of those giant inflatable bounce houses, unsteady, unpredictable, exciting. Vulnerability in its purest form. Noah must have felt it too, because he was visibly nervous.

My throat went dry. I wanted to say yes. A big, loud yes. But I needed to say it without sounding desperate, clingy, or like someone who had just collided with him for attention. In the end, all I managed was a small nod.

Noah's smile in response... that was Christmas-movie magic. He turned and started walking away, apparently satisfied with my pathetic response.

Wait. What? Just like that? No time, no place, no coordinates?

I turned and continued toward Lorenzo's apartment, the cold wind biting my cheeks, my thoughts as tangled as my hair.

And strangely, my brain had room for only one thing: Noah's unexpected invitation.

12. Doubts

No matter how high we drift among the clouds, the bills on the table always bring us back to earth. Still... floating feels wonderful while it lasts.

I never ended up going back to work. I called Lorenzo and asked to take the rest of the day off. Not because I planned to lie around doing nothing at home. If anything, I needed to get my life together. I already had plans to spend Christmas with my brother, but I wanted to have something lined up for the new year. I had to look for a job, send out résumés, all that glamorous grown-up stuff.

After a well-deserved shower, I sat on the couch in my bathrobe with my laptop balanced on my knees. Outside, the day was beautiful: bright sunshine, and little drops of melting snow dripping from the railing of the apartment balcony like a gentle metronome.

I started scrolling through job-listing websites. Nothing very inspiring in my field. Year's end is never a great time to look for work. Everyone's distracted with holidays, parties, and pretending they'll stick to their New Year's resolutions. Networking could give me some leads.

So I decided to email Marsha, my best client back before I ran away from P.F. She owned a huge horse ranch and an even bigger list of contacts. I gave her a quick update about my new life" working at my brother's café, and asked if she knew of any veterinary openings on the West Coast. I had zero intention of moving back to Alberta. Too far from Lorenzo, too far from everything I'd grown to love.

For the next two hours I fell down a rabbit hole of specialization courses, certification programs, continuing education. All of them expensive enough to make me want to lie down and rethink my existence. I had some savings, but I didn't want to burn through them without a plan, so I closed the tabs and told myself I'd revisit the idea another day.

My eyes were heavy. My head too. A nap felt like the best possible decision. I ended up sleeping for over three hours.

When I woke up, I was groggy and disoriented, the kind of nap-hangover that makes you question the date and the season. I ate a quick snack, changed into workout clothes, and decided a walk would do me good.

To avoid tourist crowding, the kind that transforms sidewalks into obstacle courses, I took a trail along the partially frozen creek. The wind was picking up, but my waterproof coat shielded me well enough. Runners, walkers, and cyclists passed by with the same determined "I'm being healthy today" energy. I tucked my hands into my pockets and kept a steady pace.

Half an hour later, I suddenly realized I was only a few blocks away from Larry's house. I considered stopping by. I had the rest of the day free. And I tried really hard not to think about whether Noah might be there.

I hesitated. Then I turned around. Maybe I should just go back to the apartment.

I took a few steps. Stopped again.

A frantic cyclist behind me rang his bell several times like he was calling me an idiot for stepping into his path. I jumped to the side, my heart racing.

And that was when I decided. I would visit Larry. And if I happened to stay a bit... maybe help with dinner... well, who knew?

Maybe, just maybe, Noah would show up.

13. Interest

My curiosity kept growing, eating away at me like slow-burning acid. What would it cost me to ask a few simple questions?

Archie greeted me at the white picket gate, tail waving with such force his whole back end wiggled. His damp paws left perfect little stamps all over my white coat, but how could anyone scold a creature so full of love and devotion?

Larry stepped onto the porch when he heard the barking.

"Sabrina, what a wonderful surprise. Noah told me you were tired and wouldn't be coming today," he said, fastening the buttons of his knitted Christmas cardigan. "Come in, come in."

Inside the living room, I said, "I had a busy morning, but I rested this afternoon. Thought I'd stop by and see if you needed anything. I can make dinner if you'd like."

Larry rubbed his hands together. "Ah, now that's an offer I can't refuse. I was just about to throw together a soup."

"Then let's get to the kitchen!" I said, more cheerful than I expected. Part of me was anxious, hoping I might see Noah; the other part was simply happy to see Larry looking a little stronger.

While I chopped onions, carrots, and potatoes at the sink, Larry sat at the table by the window, recounting his day. Soon the scent of onions sizzling in butter filled the old-fashioned kitchen. Archie licked his lips in approval, settling at my feet.

"You two are angels," Larry said out of nowhere.

I looked at him over my shoulder, wooden spoon in hand. "What do you mean?"

He chuckled, his shoulders bouncing. "Not angels in the spiritual sense. Caretaker angels. I'd have a hard time managing on my own after the scare I had. And I'm sure you and Noah have much more important things to do than look after an old man."

I couldn't speak for Noah, but my own life felt suspended in midair. I was waiting for job prospects at the hardest time of year, all my belongings boxed up in Lorenzo's garage, and my only real responsibility was helping at the café.

I added the vegetables to the pot, covered everything with water, lowered the heat, and finally sat across from Larry.

"My life's a bit stalled right now," I admitted. "Still, meeting you and Archie has been a real Christmas gift."

Archie, sprawled on the floor beside us, lifted his head at the sound of his name, then laid it back down.

And of course, I didn't add that meeting Noah had been its own unexpected gift.

We talked about our Christmas plans while the soup simmered. I told Larry I hadn't thought much about the details yet, but that I planned to spend the holiday with my brother. Larry invited me to join him and insisted I call Lorenzo to invite him too. I did, and Lorenzo accepted without hesitation.

Just as I returned to the stove to ladle soup into our bowls, the doorbell rang. Archie shot past me like a rocket, barking and wagging his tail. I opened the door and found Noah standing there, cheeks flushed from the cold, holding a white cardboard box. His familiar calm smile warmed the doorway far more than the heating vent ever could.

"Good to see you here," he said, stepping inside when I moved aside. He set the box on the entry table and pulled off his heavy coat and beanie. "I went for a walk earlier and decided to stop by."

"We're having dinner," I said. "Come on in. The soup's hot." I felt my back muscles relax.

Noah followed me down the hallway. "It smells amazing."

Larry greeted him with a warm handshake without rising from his chair. "Come, come. This soup is delicious." He was already halfway through his bowl.

Noah placed the white box on the counter. "I brought a little after-dinner surprise." He nodded toward it.

Archie barked as if he understood, then trotted off for a noisy drink of water. Dinner flowed with easy conversation and laughter, making me feel lighter than I had in days. Life is unpredictable like that—you never quite know who will cross your path. A simple act of helping an elderly man had led me to Larry. And to Noah.

After Noah and I cleaned the kitchen, while Larry supervised from the table, we opened the mysterious white box. Inside was a beautiful pie.

"I found a tiny bakery that sells every kind of pie you can imagine," Noah said with a small flourish. "The owner told me this one's the healthiest. I was thinking of Larry, still recovering. It's apple and peach, sweetened with honey. I hope you like it."

We didn't just like it. We devoured it. Even Archie got a little crumb of crust.

Then I glanced at the wall clock and felt myself deflate like a party balloon past midnight. It was time for Larry to go to bed, which meant it was also time for me to head home.

And hovering at the back of my stubborn mind was the same question: When would that coffee or tea happen with Noah? It was as if he'd forgotten. Or changed his mind.

My curiosity had moved to a new stage now. Not acid. Interest. Warm, bright, impossible-to-ignore interest.

14. The Delay

Everything seems to work against the things we want.

I left Larry's house the night before without a single word from Noah about that coffee or tea date. I went home with a heavy heart after saying goodbye to both of them. I slept well, but had a strange dream. In it, Larry lived at the North Pole making wooden toys. Not surprising, since I already saw him as the human version of Santa Claus. But Noah—and this was the funny part—came down the chimney of my house. I couldn't tell what house it was, but it looked a lot like Larry's. He brought me several presents. He wasn't dressed as Santa, just wearing ski clothes.

In the dream, I sat on the living room rug opening the gifts. They were scarves, gloves, winter gear. But the last one stood out. It was a snow globe, the kind you shake and watch the flakes fall over a Christmas scene. Attached to it was a card. I opened it, and inside was an invitation to have tea. Only I couldn't read the date or the place. Everything was smudged. I asked Noah when and where, but he climbed back up the chimney and vanished.

I woke up a little upset. The dream had felt real. But I didn't have time for fantasies. I showered and left for the café with my brother. After lunch, I got a message from Noah saying Larry had slept well through the night. I read the message, then read it again, searching for any hint of an invitation. Of course, there wasn't one.

Late in the afternoon, the invitation finally came. And thirty minutes later, I had to turn it down.

Both of Lorenzo's evening-shift employees called in sick—fever, body aches, the works. At the same time. How did that even happen?

Noah understood when I said I couldn't make it, but he didn't suggest another date. He wrote that he'd stay with Larry again and that I shouldn't worry. By the end of my shift, I was exhausted, smelled like coffee, and was in a foul mood.

When Lorenzo got home, I was already under the covers. He knocked lightly on my door, but I pretended to be asleep. Honestly, I wanted to sleep for one reason only.

To see if I could dream about Noah again.

15. Too Many Blessings?

When it rains in our little garden, it floods.

The days went by. Larry recovered so well that he started planning our Christmas celebration as if it were his daughter's wedding. He even bought a cellphone and, with Noah's help, created a group chat for the three of us to coordinate the party. Well, he coordinated; we mostly watched.

Reading Noah's messages, I saw how helpful he was. Always ready to assist Larry with anything. You could say I had a crush on him at this point. You'd be right. Or halfway right. I was somewhere between "interested" and "acting like I was twelve." I hadn't felt that way since Johnny gave me his half-eaten candy.

Don't laugh. It happened like this: he was sucking on a strawberry candy during math class in fourth grade. I had the biggest crush on him. We sat together in the back row, and honestly, I blamed him for every math issue I have to this day. I spent the entire class staring at him.

He took the red candy from his pocket, unwrapped it, and put it in his mouth. Then he looked right at me and smiled. I turned redder than the candy. For fifteen minutes he rolled the candy around his mouth with dramatic tongue movements. And then he handed it to me. I almost died. I took the candy and pretended to do the multiplication problems Ms. B. had written on the board.

Anyway, that whole story is to say that Noah made me feel the same way Johnny once did. Except I wasn't a kid anymore, and this could get serious. I wasn't expecting a half-eaten candy from Noah, but I did want his attention. And, just like that—poof—my trauma from P.F. was gone.

The truth was, since that last time I'd seen Noah at Larry's house on the day of the peach-apple pie, I hadn't run into him again. He seemed busy. Doing what, I didn't know. I had never asked what he actually did in Whistler.

Lorenzo made fun of me nonstop. He noticed my teenage attitude whenever I talked about Noah or when a message from him showed up in the group chat with Larry.

"Send him a message and ask him out for coffee. Don't wait around. Men can be slow sometimes," Lorenzo kept saying, over and over, in different ways.

"I don't know..." was always my answer.

A week before Christmas, I found my courage. I wrote to Noah:

How about we go out for hot chocolate?

His reply came at the speed of Wi-Fi.

I'm in. When and where?

He might have been slow about making the first move, but he was quick to say yes. We decided to go to the most charming inn in town the next day. Lorenzo not only gave me the day off; he ordered me to get properly dressed. I think he was tired of seeing me messy, smelling like coffee, with my hair piled up in a knot and my clothes stained with grease.

No need to say that time froze the next day. It felt like the date would never come. I did everything I could at the café to make the hours pass: cleaned, cooked, ran the register, even scrubbed the bathroom, and still, time crawled.

Finally, Lorenzo shoved me out the café door and sent me home to shower and "look presentable." I practically ran to the apartment, trying not to slip on the wet sidewalks.

The weather was good, by winter standards: clear sky, a sunset casting colors over the mountains, and crisp air. I walked home thinking about what I had in my closet.

After a long, careful shower, complete with my most expensive hair mask, I put on black pants and a cream cashmere sweater that had cost me a small fortune. I added a soft white-and-pink pashmina, draped just right. I styled my hair. It fell down my back in loose curls almost to my waist. My makeup was light, just enough to make my skin glow and eyes shine. I added earrings, a necklace, and touch of perfume. Then I chose my wool cardigan with big buttons. Of course it was pink, but a muted, elegant pink.

Voilà. I felt beautiful. Lorenzo would be proud. I took a mirror selfie and sent it to him. He replied that Noah was going to lose his mind, and that if he didn't, something was wrong with him.

I let the joke go, but I couldn't help wondering what Noah would think when he saw me. Women really are silly. But honestly, who doesn't like to feel attractive?

We had agreed to meet at the inn. Somehow it felt strange for him to pick me up, so I drove.

The inn really was charming. German-style, with brown wooden shutters, empty flower boxes, and a steep chalet roof. The pine trees out front were wrapped in Christmas lights. Everything glowed.

Or maybe I glowed when I saw Noah waiting at the door. I sighed as I climbed out of the car, trying not to slip.

Noah looked at me and smiled. "You look beautiful."

He had shaved, and I could see the clean lines of his jaw. He must have considered this a special night too; he was wearing a blazer and dress pants.

"At least I don't smell like coffee," I said, embarrassed.

"Quite the opposite."

He touched my arm and led me inside the cozy restaurant. Even though his hand only brushed my cardigan sleeve, a shiver ran down my back. If he had offered me a half-eaten red candy, I might actually have taken it.

The waitress wore traditional Bavarian clothing, her hair in two braided buns. She gave us a wide smile and led us to a table by the window near the fireplace. The sudden warmth made me slip off my coat and slide the pashmina over my shoulders. Noah placed my coat neatly on the back of my chair.

"We sometimes provide breakfast for conferences here," I told him as the server poured sparkling water into my glass.

"I thought dinner would be better than just coffee," Noah said with a quiet laugh. "You must be tired of the smell of all that."

I drank a sip of water and took in the faint aromas of food and woodsmoke. "True."

Noah smiled and shifted the conversation to Larry. He assured me Larry was doing well. My schedule at the café had been chaotic and I hadn't managed to visit him. "I have some time off tomorrow. I'll stop by," I said.

"He'll be happy."

We ordered, and soon the food arrived. We ate braised beef with warm red cabbage and talked. And I learned more about Noah.

He lived in Vancouver. Every December, he spent a month in ski towns. He owned a sportswear company that specialized in winter clothing. He even showed me his website on his phone. I was impressed by the variety of products. He said he lived with his sister.

Between dinner and dessert, I shared my story. I even told him about P.F. He listened closely and burst out laughing when I told him the story of Johnny and the red candy. I'm not sure why I brought it up, but Noah thought it was hilarious.

By dessert, I was more than interested. I was smitten.

Is love possible over a first dinner date? Maybe. It was for me.

Noah seemed at ease, too. He talked about his childhood and all the times he'd broken his arm learning to ski.

"Are you a good skier now?" I asked.

"Decent," he said, then told me about his work trips.

When the bill arrived, my heart was pounding. I had driven myself and would be going home alone. Not that I expected anything. A kiss on the cheek, maybe? But I didn't want the night to end.

Then he said:

"Want to stop by and visit Larry?"

It was late; Larry was probably getting ready for bed. But I agreed anyway. Noah surely knew what he was doing. And I wasn't going to say no.

"Let's go."

We drove separately. Soon we parked outside Larry's house.

My phone chimed. I glanced at the message and my heart sank a little, even though it shouldn't have.

Sabrina, I have a job offer for you.

How about joining my equestrian team as the veterinarian?

We're leaving for Europe in early January. — Marsha

I should've been celebrating. An opportunity like that from Marsha was impossible to refuse. No one in their right mind would turn it down.

I slipped my phone back into my bag. For tonight, I wanted to enjoy my time with Noah and pretend the message from Marsha hadn't arrived.

16. Not a Movie

In Christmas movies, the city girl always lands her dream job in the small-town guy's hometown. But life isn't a movie.

Larry greeted us with open arms. For a second, I wondered if Noah had coordinated this visit with him. But Larry was already in pajamas, which made me feel awkward. Archie trotted over with a brand-new toy, his early Christmas present, according to Larry.

Noah, being every bit the gentleman, helped me out of my cardigan and hung it on the coat rack. Before I could figure out why we were there, Larry wished us good night and disappeared down the hallway, Archie close behind.

I turned to Noah. "Shouldn't we leave? Larry's gone to bed." It sounded like the logical thing to do.

Noah shook his head and motioned for me to sit on the sofa. "I asked Larry if we could use the living room. I figured we'd want to talk." He sat beside me.

My heart started pounding again when he took my hand. So much for Lorenzo's theory that Noah was slow. I stared at him, startled. He let go.

"I didn't mean to confuse you," he said. "I just thought... the restaurant closes early, and I didn't want to lose the chance to spend more time with you. And taking you back to my hotel room wouldn't look great, would it?"

My jaw dropped. Where had this version of him been hiding?

Once I recovered, the conversation picked up again. We talked about everything: sports, cities we liked, music, even some politics. It became clearer with every topic that our values lined up. We shared the same faith.

But in the back of my mind, the job offer gnawed at me. I still needed to understand what it would require, how long I'd be gone. Most likely over six months, like every summer tournament season.

Noah talked about business school and how he started his sportswear company. He spoke with excitement, like a tap that wouldn't shut off. But it wasn't ego. It was the joy of sharing his life. With me.

The clock on the wall showed one a.m. I was tired, but I didn't dare shift my weight on the sofa, afraid he'd take it as a hint I wanted to leave. He asked about my veterinary work. I talked a lot, carefully avoiding the job proposal.

The room grew cold. Outside, snow began falling, sticking to the window. I rubbed my hands together. Noah stood and disappeared down the hallway. I craned my neck, trying to see where he went. Maybe the bathroom?

He returned with a blanket and draped it over my shoulders. "I think the heating in this house needs help. I froze last night too. Larry sleeps under a mountain of blankets with Archie glued to his side."

"It's funny how attached we've gotten to him," I said. "We act like his grandkids." I laughed and pulled the blanket closer.

Noah shook his head slightly. Something was bothering him. He looked down at the floor, then back up at me.

"Sabrina, I've been wondering about something."

I raised my eyebrows. "Yes?"

"From what I understand, you love your work. You came here because of the stalker. And after that? What's the plan? I mean... you won't stay working in the café forever, right?"

Now *I* looked at the floor. Whatever I said next could ruin the moment. Ruin the possibility of getting to know Noah better. Maybe even ruin something I was just beginning to hope for.

"I don't want to pry," he added.

I shook my head. "You're not. I... actually..."

"If you'd rather not talk about it, that's okay."

I let out a breath. "I got a job offer today. From a former client." Then I told him about the European tournament.

The room fell still, except for the faint ticking of Larry's clock on the wall.

He leaned back a little, eyes dropping to the blanket over my shoulders. His jaw tightened a little, but enough for me to notice. "I see. And how long would you be away?"

"I'm not sure yet. At least six months. We train in early spring, then the competitions. Summer is the busiest period."

Real life wasn't a movie. I had bills. A career. A future to consider. I couldn't give all that up for some idea I had that maybe Noah and I were something.

"I'm happy for you," he said.

A sentence that should have brought joy instead cracked something inside me. What was I expecting? That he'd beg me to stay?

"Thank you," I answered, without an ounce of excitement.

What happened next took me completely off guard.

17. With a Heavy Heart

Was there a way to stop time?

I don't know exactly what happened between one breath and the next. One moment I was sitting beside Noah on Larry's sofa, the blanket still warm around my shoulders. The next, I was in his arms and his mouth was on mine.

I can't remember who leaned in first. I just remember the shock. Not from the kiss (believe me, *that* part was incredible), but from how sudden it happened.

I melted instantly, like a scoop of ice cream on a July sidewalk.

For a split second, I almost let myself slip into the fantasy, the sweet Christmas-movie version of my life. The one where the girl gives up the big job to stay with the quiet, kind guy who smelled good and kissed like that.

But I couldn't. Not in real life.

Noah smelled clean and warm, like winter air mixed with something woodsy. His skin was soft, his hands strong, and his kiss! His kiss hit me in a place no one had ever reached until now.

But it ended as abruptly as it had begun, leaving a quiet ache in me.

I pulled the blanket back around me, shaking, not only from the cold. My whole body demanded more.

Noah let out a long breath and ran a hand across his forehead. "If I say I didn't want to do that, I'd be lying," he said. "I just didn't think I'd actually get the courage to kiss you." He shook his head, like brushing away a rogue thought. "I honestly thought you'd slap me."

The comment surprised me. "Why would I do that?"

"You didn't... give me much signal," he said with a nervous laugh.

Fair enough. I'd been running away from P.F. and from anything that resembled romantic involvement. "I guess I didn't."

"But hey, I survived the slap I didn't get," Noah said.

I reached out and gently touched his cheek. "I wouldn't hit you."

He took my hand and kissed my palm. Then he threaded his fingers through mine, holding them there like he didn't want to let go.

We talked a while longer, our hands joined, both of us carefully stepping around the subject of my departure. The clock struck two a.m. before I could admit to myself that my eyes were barely staying open. I'd have to work in a few hours.

Noah helped me into my cardigan, patient and gentle, like he was afraid the moment might end if he moved too fast. He walked me to my car, the snow crunching softly under our boots. He opened the door for me and bent down so we were face-to-face.

"I bet Larry would have some good advice for us," he said.

I sighed. "I'm sure he would."

He kissed my cheek—soft, warm, lingering just enough for my breath to catch. Then he closed the door.

It took me a full ten seconds to find the ignition. When I drove away, the taste of his kiss still on my lips. The sensation of his soft touch on my neck spreading like wildfire through my body. My heart ached.

And the weight of the separation already sat heavy on my chest.

18. Indecent Proposal

Was I being greedy or just careful?

Christmas was two days away. With my curiosity about Noah finally satisfied, I found myself delaying my reply to Marsha about the equestrian team. As expected, there wasn't a single job posting that fit my experience.

A piece of advice from my mother resurfaced at just the right moment: *Don't depend on anyone financially.* Not because families or partners shouldn't support each other, she had said, but because even the healthiest relationships face lean seasons. And the more capable hands contributing, the easier it is to make it through. I grew up with that mindset.

Yes, my brother was helping me now, and yes, if I were in trouble, I could lean on my parents. But my mother's point still stood—I had to take my career seriously, even if that meant being far from where I wanted to be.

After the night of my date with Noah, after the sublime kiss, I had planned to talk to Larry and ask for his advice. What I really wished for was the impossible: to keep this careful, brand-new thing with Noah alive and still say yes to the job. But every time I tried to map it out in my head, the lines crossed in all the wrong places.

That cold, cloudy morning, after a long shower, I sat on my bed and emailed Marsha asking for more details. I ate a light breakfast, got dressed, and glanced at my inbox one last time before leaving. And there it was: the offer. A loud gasp escaped me. The offer was almost indecent, in the best way.

I'd be away for a full year, traveling with the team, and I'd come back with my savings account overflowing. I widened my eyes at the number. I knew the equestrian world involved money, but I hadn't expected that many zeros.

A dream I'd carried for years surfaced immediately: opening my own vet clinic. My hands trembled as I closed the laptop. I put on my boots, and rushed to the café.

The rest of the day passed like a movie on fast-forward. I worked at the register, behind the counter, and in the kitchen without really thinking. Lorenzo kept glancing at me, but the Christmas rush didn't give us a chance to talk.

That night, I went to Larry's house. He watched me prepare chicken noodle soup. Sitting at the table, he observed me peeling potatoes and carrots. Archie slept beside him, worried only about when his next meal would be.

The knife slipped on the cutting board and nicked my finger. I rinsed it under the tap, wrapped it in a piece of paper towel, and when I turned around, Larry gestured for me to sit across from him. I obeyed.

"I can tell you're restless," he said. "And I get it. You probably don't want to unload your worries on an old man whose biggest goal in life is to stay alive and mostly pain-free." He smiled gently.

I listened.

He continued:

"When we're young, we're impatient. We want everything overnight. With time, we learn the truth from the Bible that each day has enough troubles, so we should not worry about tomorrow. We can't push time forward or drag it back. Nothing grows without time. Anything rushed ends up poorly done."

I let his words sink in. I knew they were true. I believed them. But how to apply that truth to the mess in my head and heart?

Larry looked at me, his calm blue eyes steady. "It's not one thing or the other, Sabrina. It's not your job or Noah."

How did he know what I was wrestling with? Had Noah said something? It didn't matter. I wanted to hear him out.

"There are things time doesn't ruin," he said. "Love, for example. I loved my Agnes, and I'll love her until the day I go to heaven to join her." He laughed. "Not sure if we'll recognize each other there. Doesn't matter. We'll be in the same place. That's enough." He leaned back, still watching me. "Right now, you and Noah are in the same place. I don't mean Whistler or Canada. I mean Earth. You young people trust your phones more than anything, but you don't believe you can stay connected while being apart." His laugh made Archie lift his ears.

"So you think I should take the job?" I asked, still not certain how he knew about it.

"Not my decision," Larry replied. "Who am I to say? At my age, I've learned people rarely follow advice anyway. They follow their immediate desires. They make excuses to justify decisions, sometimes foolish ones. Some even spiritualize their choices, and later they reap bitter fruit. Not saying it is you, but I learned to share the truth from the Bible and let the person plant the seed where they want. Fertile or barren soil." He shrugged. "So I'm telling you what a long life has taught me. There is nothing new under the sun."

His words made sense. I wanted the immediate desire, which was staying close to Noah. But my bank account was limited, and I didn't want to depend on my brother or abandon my career.

I stood, finished the soup, and realized I still had no idea what I was going to do. I was afraid.

19. The Snow Globes

Was it possible for two people to have the same dream?

Christmas Eve was full of surprises. I woke up and Lorenzo announced I would have the entire day off. I didn't understand why at first, but I thanked him anyway. Only later did everything make sense.

With unexpected free time and my mind running in circles, I walked down the busy village and bought a gift for Noah. I had no idea what he liked, so I chose something symbolic: a small snow globe with a Christmas village inside, just like the one in my dream. It was simple, but meaningful.

I stopped by Larry's house and found his neighbor helping out with her two teen grandkids. She was preparing lunch while the kids cleaned up the living room. We chatted a bit, and she explained Larry had gone to the grocery store. Relieved, I headed home. As soon as I closed the apartment door, my phone rang.

It was Noah.

My stomach flipped when he asked if I wanted to go out that afternoon. The Christmas celebration at Larry's would be the next day, starting at lunch and, according to him, lasting until everyone was too full to move. So I accepted. He only added, "Wear something warm and comfortable."

When Noah called again to say he'd pick me up in twenty minutes, I ran to my room. I grabbed my red hat, gloves, and scarf. I put on my white winter coat—very Christmas-appropriate—and slipped his gift into my bag. I didn't want to give it to him in front of Larry, Lorenzo, and Diana, Noah's sister, who would be arriving early the next morning.

Outside, Noah greeted me with a hug and opened the car door. We drove along a winding road between snow-laden trees until a ranch appeared. I smiled instantly when I saw the magnificent Percheron horses. I hadn't realized how much I missed being around them until that exact moment.

Noah parked, and we walked toward a log cabin. Tourists of every kind went in and out, laughing with red cheeks and cold noses. Noah spoke to an attendant, who pointed us toward a side door.

The winter sun was already dipping when he took my hand and led me into a large barn. Inside, a mighty Percheron stood hitched to a sleigh. Noah helped me onto one. The coachman greeted us and handed us a thick blanket. We snuggled under it, and the sleigh pulled out of the barn. The bells around the horse's collar jingled like our own private Christmas carol as we glided through the white fields. The sky looked like black velvet torn open by stars.

Noah slid an arm around my shoulders. "Merry Christmas Eve, Sabrina."

"Merry Christmas Eve, Noah." A tight knot formed in my throat. It felt more like a goodbye than a holiday greeting.

We rode in quiet for a while, listening only to the bells. I rested my head on his shoulder and stared up at the sky. Larry had been right: I kept wanting to put my immediate desire first. Before I could sink too deep into worry, Noah spoke, as if he'd climbed right into my thoughts.

"Sabrina, I've been thinking a lot about you, about me. To be honest, I wasn't even planning to come to Whistler. I was supposed to fly to Montreal. But at the last minute, the client canceled, so I came here instead." His fingers brushed my cheek gently. "And that's when I met this wonderful, slightly grumpy woman at Aspen Lodge." I laughed, and he went on, "It felt like you and I had an appointment we didn't know about. We both came here because we had no choice, maybe because something bigger wanted us in the same place. Someone bigger." He paused and exhaled. "I know you're torn. I am too. I don't want you to go. But I can't and shouldn't stand in the way of this incredible opportunity."

His words stung. Was he telling me to take the job? And what about us?

"We'll have our time," he said, answering the question I hadn't asked aloud. "Larry's right: you young people trust your phones for everything except what they're actually best at: staying connected." He chuckled, and I joined him. "And I saw your eyes light up when you looked at those horses. That's your gift, Sabrina. Your calling."

I leaned into him even more and pulled the blanket closer to my chin. "I wish I could stay close to you."

"Who says you won't?"

I blinked. "I don't understand."

"We might be apart physically, but not emotionally. A year goes by fast. And you'll be home by next Christmas."

His words sank in softly. I thought of what Larry had said about not rushing time. Maybe patience really could give me the best of both worlds.

Then Noah shifted and reached into his coat pocket. He pulled out a small wrapped package. "For you."

The bells around the horse's neck almost seemed to play a melody of their own. I opened the package and my gloved hand flew to my face.

A snow globe. Exactly like the one he didn't know I had bought for him.

"I didn't expect that reaction," he said gently. "It's just a small gift. I don't know your taste yet but I'd like to."

I reached into my bag and handed him my package. Noah laughed when he saw the identical snow globe.

"Some things really do feel written in the heavens," he said, pointing to the glittering sky. "There's our answer."

Yes.

Even with tears in my eyes, we had our answer.

And for the first time since everything began, it felt like the right one.

20. The End is Just the Beginning

We really can't know what's written in the heavens.

Well, that's how my best story began. Exactly—began. That was only the first chapter of many beautiful ones and one not so beautiful.

The day after my sleigh ride with Noah, we celebrated Christmas. Lorenzo and Diana talked nonstop, and I suspected from the very beginning that their story was about to start too.

Larry was practically glowing with excitement. He served a huge feast and told stories of Christmases past. He spoke about Agnes and brought us all to tears.

Archie, whom Larry called "the reason the three of us ever met," trotted between our legs trying to charm extra pieces of turkey out of anyone who made eye contact.

Everyone celebrated with me when I told them about the new job that would take me away for a full year. Noah was steady, reassuring. He kept telling me, "I'll see you next Christmas."

The festivities wound down, and in early January I hugged Lorenzo goodbye and headed to the airport. Noah drove me down the mountain toward Vancouver.

Our goodbye was painful, but the months that followed were full of victories for both of us. His company grew. And in October, while I was in France, Lorenzo and Diana called to say they were engaged. They whispered that Noah was counting the days to see me again.

I couldn't bear the wait anymore. Every day apart stretched a little thinner, a little tighter. We talked almost every day, sometimes sharing big news, sometimes nothing at all. Sometimes just breathing together on the phone. We shared everything, and nothing, and somehow it all meant the world.

But then came the one discordant note. The news of Larry's passing.

Lorenzo was the one who told me. He had made a habit of visiting Larry every week, and it was the neighbor who found him collapsed in the front yard, with Archie crying at his side.

I called Noah the moment I could speak. We cried together, long and without shame. We remembered that first dinner in Larry's storybook house, the way he had folded us into his world as if we belonged there all along. We laughed through the tears at his joy, his sweetness, his love for Agnes. And in the end, we found comfort in the "not-advice" he'd given us.

A few days before my return to Canada, Noah called with an unbelievable message: Larry had left the storybook house to both of us. I cried the whole night. Larry had been more than a friend—he'd been our grandfather, our counselor, our inspiration.

On December twentieth, I boarded my flight home, home to familiar skies, and home to the man who had waited for me. When I stepped into the arrivals hall, I spotted Noah, standing tall with a massive bouquet of flowers. As soon as he saw me, his whole face lit up. He moved so quickly that petals spilled from the bouquet and scattered in a trail behind him. Passengers flowed around us, annoyed, amused. I didn't care. Noah reached me, gathered me into his arms, and held on like he'd been saving that hug for months. And then he kissed me—warm, a *welcome home* pressed right against my lips.

As we drove back up the mountain toward Whistler, snow tapping against the windshield, Noah suddenly pulled over, stepped out of the car, and reached for me.

With the breathtaking snow-capped mountains behind him, he knelt in the snow, opened a small velvet box, and revealed an engagement ring. Right there, under the falling flakes, we held each other and kissed.

Larry had been right. We never tried to rush time. And the rewards came. During that year apart, Noah and I didn't drift; we grew closer. The distance didn't stop us. It did the opposite. Sometimes being physically near could get in the way of truly seeing someone's soul. In that year, we opened ours completely.

Before seeing Lorenzo, Diana, and my parents, who had flown from Florida to spend Christmas with their children and meet their future son- and daughter-in-law, Noah and I stopped at Larry's house.

Our inheritance. Our home.

We opened the door, and the first thing we noticed was the quiet. Archie had been adopted by the neighbor, but his toys were still scattered on the floor. Larry would've wanted it that way.

On top of the old dining-room cabinet, the photos of Agnes remained. I studied each one and startled at a new picture with a golden frame. Noah and I stood in front of the Christmas tree Larry had put up for our celebration the year before. Beside the photo sat a snow globe and a small envelope.

My shoulders shook as I cried. Noah gently took the envelope from my hand and read:

"Everything has its proper time. Some things return to us, even when distance gets in the way. Love does that. I've left this world to meet my God and my Agnes.

Sabrina and Noah, live your lives with love. You will never be disappointed."

Noah pulled me close, and I heard his quiet crying against my shoulder. Our words of comfort slowly turned into words of love, the same words we had spoken for months over the phone.

We pulled apart, and I held Larry's letter in my hands.

With a solemn voice, I said, "Thank you, my dear friend. We love you."

The End

www.ingramcontent.com/pod-product-compliance
Lightning Source LLC
Chambersburg PA
CBHW070640130626
46555CB00006B/2638